In memory of my grandmother Florence Bullard,
who taught me that the best gift comes from the heart and hands.

And to Annie and Eliza, nimble-fingered knitters extraordinaire.

All rights reserved. Published in the United States by Schwartz & Wade Books,

an imprint of Random House Children's Books, a division of Penguin Random House LLC, New York.

Schwartz & Wade Books and the colophon are trademarks of Penguin Random House LLC.

Visit us on the Web! rhcbooks.com

Educators and librarians, for a variety of teaching tools, visit us at RHTeachersLibrarians.com

Library of Congress Cataloging-in-Publication Data is available upon request.

ISBN 978-0-593-17442-5 (hardcover) — ISBN 978-0-593-17443-2 (lib. bdg.)

ISBN 978-0-593-17444-9 (ebook)

The text of this book is set in 17-point Century Schoolbook.

The illustrations were created digitally in the Procreate app.

MANUFACTURED IN CHINA

2 4 6 8 10 9 7 5 3

First Edition

Mistletoe

A Christmas Story

by Tad Hills

schwartz & wade books · new york

Mistletoe greets the chilly morning. Snow is falling.
What a beautiful day! Finally, it feels like Christmas, she thinks.

By the time she gets to Norwell's house, the snow is almost up to her knees.

"Norwell, come out! It's SNOWING!"

Mistletoe calls.

Norwell watches Mistletoe.
It sure looks cold out there, Norwell says
to himself. *Too cold for this elephant.*

"Mistletoe, it's cold out there. Why don't you
come in? Sit by the fire and have some tea!"

"Just a drop for me, and a cookie crumb, please," says Mistletoe. "And after tea we can go for a walk in the snow."

Norwell and Mistletoe sit by the warm and toasty fire.

"Isn't this nice, Mistletoe?" asks Norwell.

"Oh, yes, indeed it is," Mistletoe agrees, "but wouldn't it also be nice to take a stroll in the snow?"

Later Mistletoe helps Norwell decorate his tree.

"After we top it off with a star, can we go out and catch snowflakes on our tongues?" says Mistletoe.

"Hmmm, I don't know." Norwell walks to the window. He watches the snow fall. *"Brrrr,"* he says. "It looks even colder out there now, Mistletoe. I think I'll stay home, where it's cozy."

So Mistletoe puts on her hat, coat, scarf, and mittens and sets out on her walk home. She soon finds herself in a field of snow. As evening approaches, the world turns blue. She stops. She is as quiet and still as she has ever been.

Norwell should be here with me
to listen to the falling snow, she thinks.
Suddenly she has an idea.

Mistletoe cannot
get home fast enough.

When she gets inside, she tosses
off her snow-covered clothes,

climbs into her attic, and finds just what she needs.

She gathers her yarn, settles in with her knitting needles, and gets to work.

You can never have too much yarn, she says to herself.

Mistletoe knits whenever she can. She knits when the sun comes up and when the sun is down.

She knits while she reads.

She knits while she makes cookies for Santa.

She even knits in the bath (which isn't easy).

Days pass. Christmas nears.

Mistletoe knits and knits, using every bit of yarn she can find around her house.

Mistletoe realizes two things: one, sometimes you *don't* have enough yarn, and two, elephants are big!

She stops at her favorite shop and brings home as much yarn as she can.

Finally, on Christmas Eve, Mistletoe puts down her
knitting needles. Her fingers are tired. Her work is done.
She watches the snow fall outside her window and
thinks of Norwell. "Ah, Christmas." She smiles.

Then Mistletoe nestles into her
soft knitting, and falls into a deep sleep.

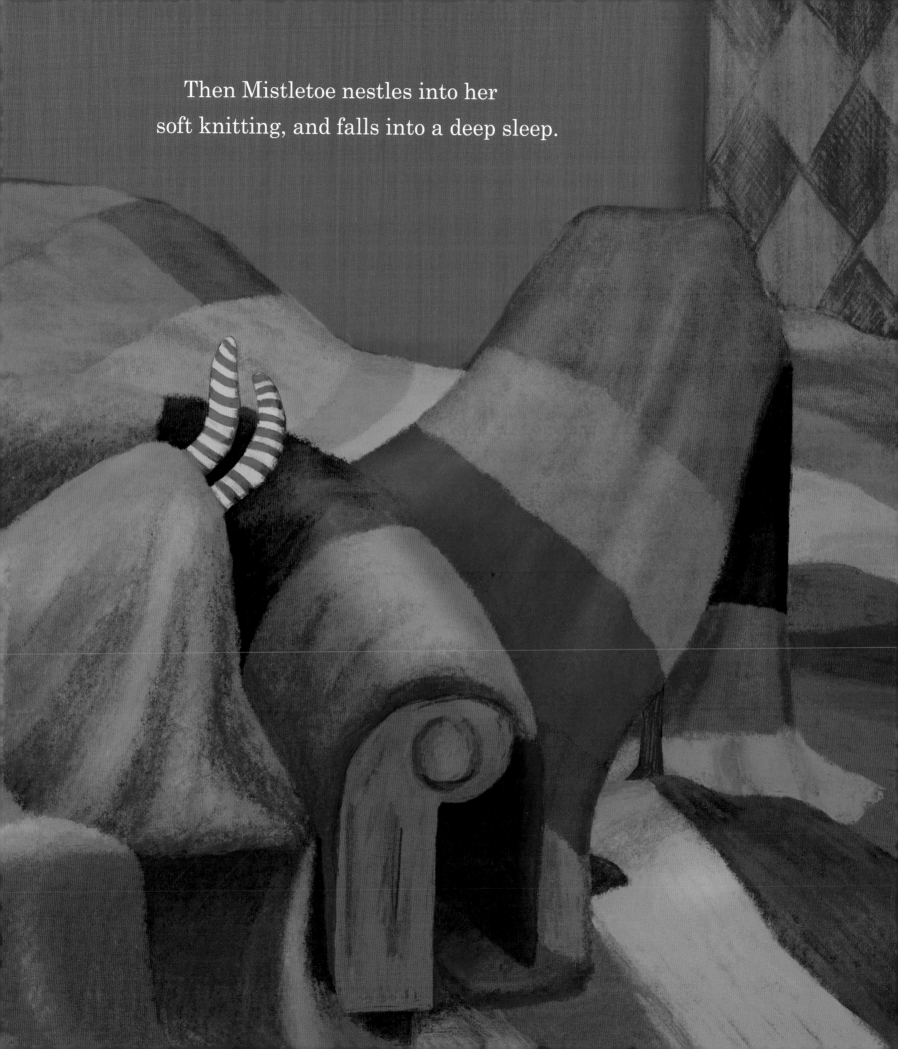

The next morning, Mistletoe opens her eyes as the sun fills her living room. Christmas is here!

The cookies are gone, and beautifully wrapped gifts have been left under the tree.

"Thank you, Santa," she calls up the chimney. "Merry Christmas!"

Opening her presents will have to wait,
though, because Mistletoe has other plans.
First she puts on her Christmas dress.

Then she carefully folds
the gift she has made for
Norwell, adds a red ribbon,

and squeezes the gift
through the front door.

Mistletoe pulls the heavy gift behind her.

"Merry Christmas, Norwell!
I have something for you,"

she calls when she reaches her friend's house.

"Merry Christmas, Mistletoe," Norwell says. "Come in, come in! I have something special for you too."

Norwell hands Mistletoe
the most beautifully wrapped
package she has ever seen.

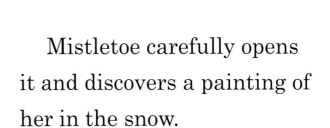

Mistletoe carefully opens
it and discovers a painting of
her in the snow.
   "It's perfect, Norwell."
   "You do love snow, Mistletoe."
   "Indeed I do!"

When it's Norwell's turn to open his gift, Mistletoe asks,
"Do you know what it is, Norwell?"

"I don't know what it is, but I love it!"

"Oh, Mistletoe, it is so colorful and soft!" Norwell exclaims. "It will keep you toasty and warm," Mistletoe tells Norwell, ". . . outside in the snow!"

"You do like to be toasty and
warm, Norwell," said Mistletoe.
"Indeed I do!" agreed Norwell.

And he was.